Tomorrow is Yesterday

JESSIE WINTERSPRING

For my husband who gets bored reading long fiction. Is this short enough for you?

"Time is precious – spend it wisely"

- Anonymous

Part one

-Chicago 1972-

For Twilight, the world was a crappy place to live in. Some enjoyed living blissfully in the light, while she and others like her lived in the shadows, but everyone pushed through to survive.

"Hey, Miss, do you want some smoke?"

Twilight threw a glance at the dubious man wearing a light brown coat and smiled. Obviously, the man took it as a sign of agreement and approached her from the dark area of the street. "I've got plenty of supply today. I can give you a discount if you'll recommend me to others."

"Sure. But is it okay to buy just a few? I'm new here and just want to try a small amount." Twilight faked another smile and reached for the wallet in her pocket. All she wanted was to kick the man in his balls and run from this stinking dark alley plagued by people high from things she didn't even want to imagine.

The man eyed Twilight with suspicion, but she had a mission, and the last thing she wanted was to have him become suspicious of her. She might not be the best actress, but she could scrape by when needed.

Growing up an orphan, she'd survived for eighteen years on the few skills she possessed and was determined not to fail now. She stood her ground, acting as though she wanted to keep everything quiet. This appeared to persuade him. From his pocket, he pulled out an item resembling a regular cigarette and a small packet of tablets.

The man began describing the drug's various effects, but Twilight was indifferent to the details. She took one of the drug, paid more than the asking price, and left.

She went home, flushed it down her toilet, and returned there each night for a week until she slowly got familiar with a few people. Enough so they would think she was no danger to them.

"Gardo, may I ask you a question?" she asked him after paying for the same product.

"Of course you can. What is it? A friend needs help?"

She smiled. "No, actually, I was wondering if you ever wonder why I keep coming back here."

He laughed. "Well, I did. But I figured you must be some troubled rich girl, right? I've seen lots of you here before, but so far, you're the only one who seemed to know how to hold it together."

She supposed she could pass as a rich girl with her fiery red hair and emerald color· eyes. It was the characteristic that her customers loved. "I'm not a troubled rich girl."

His face turned serious. "You're not going to tell me that you're some undercover cop, are you?"

"No. Actually, I'm looking for someone."

Gardo ruffled his short hair and tossed his smoke on the ground. "You got close to me after finding out I know a lot, did you?"

"Yes."

"And you never use any of the stuff you bought."

"Yes."

Gardo grabbed the collar of her blouse and pinned her against the wall. People nearby who were awake enough to understand that something was wrong warily walked off. "Who are you? What do you want?"

"I'm no one you need to be careful with, Gardo. You should know that by now." He didn't loosen his grip. Twilight continued, "I'm just a prostitute looking for my brother. His name is Ellio, he's fourteen. Bushy brown hair, blue eyes, skinny and about this tall..." She lifted her hands above her head. "According to some people I've been asking, they last saw him in this area getting beat up by the Faceless—"

Gardo covered her mouth and said, "Don't mention their names here." Then he let her go and signaled her to follow him

Twilight followed Gardo toward the largest park in the city, which was also known to be the hangout of people with twisted minds at night. He stopped in front of a dry fountain.

"This is where I last saw him a month ago."

Blood rushed to Twilight's head as she remembered the time he ran off following a major argument. "At first, I mistook him for a skinny street kid," Gardo said. He tried to recruit him, but Ellio declined, wanting to know who led the local gang. Gardo glanced around uneasily, scratching his head. "I seriously wanted to stop him, but he was an unlucky kid."

Sensing where the story was headed, Twilight remained quiet, listening intently.

Gardo went on. "That night, the gang members interrupted our talk and tried to scare your brother by saying he wasn't worth their boss' time. But he stood his ground, even though he was clearly scared. He bravely asked them to take him to their leader, offering information on their rivals, the Crocodile gang, in return for your freedom. Gardo shook his head. Twilight felt light-headed at the information and it took all her might not to fall. "It was a reckless move from your brother. They just laughed and attacked him. I was scared, too. I started to walk away when I saw one pull out a gun, but..."

"But what?" Twilight stared at him, hoping that he would say that Ellio got away.

Gardo frowned and said the most incomprehensible thing. "He disappeared."

"What do you mean, disappeared? He managed to run away? Is that it?"

"No, disappeared. Vanished. Puffed. Before they killed him, the ground swallowed your brother, together with all the other Faceless group members."

Twilight frowned. "Huh?"

A suspicious man passed by and looked at them. "Sorry

about this," she heard Gardo whisper before he pushed her away. "I told you already. Pay me either by cash or nothing! I don't exchange pleasure for my product! Show up when you have more bucks!"

With that, Gardo left and made a respectful bow to the man. The man acknowledged him with a nod and turned his attention to her. Trying not to meet the man's eyes, she hung her head in shame. Even though she wasn't part of the Crocodile gang, they still had control over her. She had to keep her identity hidden—being discovered by the Faceless group could mean a fate worse than death. Holding on to hope was crucial, especially now that she had a glimmer of hope that Ellio might still be out there, alive.

Long after Gardo was gone, Twilight was still there, looking at the dry fountain as she sat on the cobblestone, hugging her knees. The night seemed endless as she watched the passersby from the darkness. The feeling of loneliness that she hadn't felt ever since she found Ellio had returned tenfold now that she knew what had happened.

Twilight knew nothing where she came from. The first guardian she knew was a homeless woman raised until she was five. She never failed to remind Twilight to be grateful for her generosity of taking her, and naming her, a baby thrown in the trash. The woman was killed by a man from the crocodile gang who took her with him. He used her to beg on the street and raped her as soon as she reached puberty. He died in a gang fight and the crocodile gang gave her his home and kept her on a leash. At thirteen, she felt like an adult. She gets paid for selling herself and pays her apartment rent and protection fee to the gang.

She never imagined that the snotty street boy she brought

home with her on a whim to celebrate her freedom would come to mean so much to her and make her feel so lost.

Behind his mischievousness, Ellio was faithful and good-hearted. They may have started as strangers, but they grew to live as a family. She just never realized how important his existence had become until he walked out of her house that day after they argued about her job. She can still see him clearly now as he stood by the kitchen table, his arm muscles tensing as his fists clenched at his sides, the determination to make her see his point. "You can't do this anymore, Twilight," he pleaded, his blue eyes filled with worry and frustration.

"I don't need you telling me what to do, Ellio. You're too young to support us both," she shot back, her hands planted firmly on her hips.

"But you were younger than I am now when you took me in," Ellio countered, his voice quivering slightly. "You've done enough. It's my turn now."

The defiant stance she held slackened. She moved across the kitchen table and sat down. "You think you can suddenly play the grown-up, Ellio?"

"I've been doing it already, haven't I? Between providing food and mending clothes," Ellio pressed on, stepping closer to her. The silence filled the room, broken only by the occasional drip from a broken water tap.

"That... That doesn't count," she retorted, unable to explain why she felt angry and happy at the same time. No one wanted to take care of her without something in exchange, and Ellio wanting to take care of her scared her. At fourteen, he was taller than her, and sometimes he looked at her like someone else. Almost like the way a man would. However, unlike those who gaze at her with pure lust, Ellio's eyes were warm and kind. His actions often made her feel as if he wanted to cradle her. It comforted her and the thought of him supporting her terrified her because that might change him. Now she'd lost him instead.

She supposed she'd taken it for granted that they would always be together. Now, she realized how wrong she was. She would give her life to see him again and apologize.

Just after thinking that, Twilight suddenly felt the ground beneath her soften. She found herself sinking quickly. Surprised, it took her a while before she tried to wiggle out and call for help, but there was no one around. The ground behaved as if it was quicksand. The more she struggled, the faster she sank.

Twilight gave up resisting when the ground was up to her nose and choking her. She closed her eyes, silently wishing that she could have seen Ellio before she died.

Part two

The next time she came to her senses, Twilight whiffed the smell of cool fresh air. She felt soft grass beneath her and the gentle sound of splashing water as if it were lightly raining in a pond.

Oh, what a good feeling, she thought, wanting to just lie there and bask in the peacefulness she had never felt before.

"Twilight."

Her eyes shot open at the familiar gentleness, yet the unfamiliar voice of a man. Twilight sat up and saw the blinding daylight and that she was lying on the grass, surrounded by tall green trees. Her eyes first landed on the familiar fountain, except it was now filled with water, a small geyser spraying up from the center of the basin, which then splashed the stones below. She then turned to the presence beside her and saw a pair of brilliant blue eyes.

"Ellio!" she called out happily but paused before hugging him when she realized that the person with her couldn't be him. He's an adult guy, probably more than a decade older than Ellio.

The man laughed and pulled her close. "Twilight! It's me."

"Who?"

"Don't be stubborn, Twilight." The man set her free and she

felt a twinge of disappointment. It was a refreshing feeling for her to be hugged by a man just for the joy of it, not because he needed her for sex. "You know who I am. You just called my name."

Yes, in the corner of Twilight's mind, she did have a feeling that the man was right. The rational part refused to accept it. It didn't matter how many similarities they shared. Twilight let out a small laugh. He did the same. Soon they were both laughing like two insane people before Twilight furiously stood up and hit him.

"Don't you dare make fun of me! You're not my brother!"

"I was never your brother!" The man's face turned severe as he stood up and towered over her. Twilight's survival instincts wanted her to cower down and apologize. Still, she stood her ground and looked straight into his eyes.

"You might have thought of me that way, but I never saw you as my sister, Twilight."

The wind blew his bushy brown hair, and Twilight immediately noticed the large scar running from his forehead down to his ears.

Twilight reached up to his face and traced the scar he received from the member of the crocodile gang after he tried to prevent them from hurting her when he was nine. This happened a short time after she took him in. "Ellio."

"Yes, I am." Ellio's face mellowed. His eyes flickered just as she remembered.

Twilight brought her hands back to her sides. "But how? I mean, you're supposed to be a small boy."

"I've grown."

"A scrawny fourteen-year-old!"

"Yes, I've aged ten years and a bit more. I've also grown some muscles. Want to see them?"

"You don't make sense! And where are we?"

Ellio just laughed and put his arm around Twilight's shoulders. "Let's go to my place so that I can tell you all about it."

Ellio brought her to a big mansion not far from the fountain. He invited her into the luxurious living room three times as big as her own apartment. After the servant served them coffee and biscuits, Ellio sat beside her and told Twilight his almost unbelievable story.

He said that after the incident, which he recounted just as Gardo had described, he found himself sucked down into the ground and woke up in the exact same place she did.

"I don't know how it happened, but the men who were dragged down with me were dead." Ellio sipped his coffee and rubbed the rim with his thumb. It was so weird for her to see him as a fully grown adult and yet still retaining the little habits when he was younger. "I wandered around the place for hours, hoping to get to the city, but I collapsed from hunger. By the time I woke up... I was in this house." A warm smile spread across Ellio's face. He told her that the mansion was owned by a loving couple, who informed him that he was sixty-three years back in time. "I don't know if they really believed my story, but, yeah, after a while, it was proved that they were right."

"Wait, so you're saying that we're in...." Twilight did the math. "The year 1909?"

"No, that was the time when I was thrown here. That was fourteen years ago."

"Oh, so then now is...." She tried to calculate again, but her mind was starting to spin.

"It's 1923."

Twilight laughed. "Oh right, right." She'd never been in school, and math wasn't exactly what she was good at. The little knowledge she had was gained from some generous customers who lent her a bit of their time after sex. Before the Crocodile gang took her in and turned her into their slave, she was a street kid. "I-if we're really back in time... w-we're free."

"Yes. We are. When I first figured that out, I wanted to return to the future immediately."

Twilight's eyes widened in disbelief. "Why?" She looked around them and outside the large windows. "Even a fool could tell that you have a much better life here!"

"You're right, but you weren't here with me." Ellio looked at her in a way that bothered her heart. "All these years, there wasn't a day when I didn't visit the place you came from, hoping to get back and bring you back here. As the years went by, I started losing hope, but seeing you sleeping there today was the highlight of my life." Ellio stood up and put his hands on her sides, trapping her in front of him. "In fact, it's actually good that you ended up here and now, so I wouldn't have to make you wait for me to grow."

"What are you—"

He took her chin and made her look up. "Twilight, I'm still the boy you helped, but I'm no longer helpless. I'm a man now. A man who's has been waiting to confess his love to you all this time."

Twilight swallowed as she gazed at Ellio's serious face. Yeah, he might be the same person as the boy she brought home, but he was no longer the same boy. He looked like a man, talked like a man, and moved like a man. Someone familiar, yet also a stranger.

Unable to continue looking at him, Twilight avoided his eyes and caught a glimpse of familiar names that made her tense up. Even just reading them sent chills down her spine. Ellio noticed it too and freed her. He went to where the list was and plopped it down on the coffee table in front of her.

Twilight's hand shook as she reached out for the paper and saw a strikethrough on the names Alfie and Caldwell. They were the names of the Faceless and Crocodile gang leaders in the future. "W-Why do you have this list?" A horrible suspicion crept up on her, which got even worse after hearing his hearty laugh.

"I killed them so that they won't grow up and build those gangs."

Twilight's stomach lurched as the image of Ellio murdering someone flashed in her mind. She didn't rescue him from the gutter just to make him into another criminal.

"Is that what you expected me to say?"

"Huh?" A lone tear dropped from Twilight eyes onto the list.

Ellio sighed. He looked hurt as he said, "But I can't blame you. Even I had that urge when I first met them, but I'm not stopping so low as to murder kids." He offered his hand to Twilight.

Twilight took it and let him guide her out of the living room.

He asked one of the maids where Alfie and Caldwell were and headed to the pool, still holding her hand.

There at the kid's pool, two boys of three and five were enjoying themselves in the water. The moment they noticed them, the boys waved.

The oldest one hurriedly approached them and studied Twilight with his sharp gray eyes that made her quiver in both fear and anger. He looked unmistakably like his future self.

"Don't. He's an innocent kid."

Twilight gazed up to Ellio, who gave her hand a squeeze as he restrained her. True to his word, everything suddenly cleared up, and Twilight saw that Caldwell had a soft smile as he looked up to her. There was not a trace of the cruelty that she knew from his future self in his eyes, only curiosity as he observed their linked hands.

"Daddy? Is she your girlfriend?"

"D-Daddy?" Twilight repeated. Ellio smiled at her and answered Caldwell.

"Not yet, but I hope to ask her."

"Oh, she's going to be our mom?"

"What? There's no—"

Ellio's laughter drowned her words. He ruffled Caldwell's hair. "Go back to your brother for now, okay?"

Caldwell beamed at Ellio and politely smiled at Twilight, who awkwardly returned the gesture.

After Caldwell left, Ellio once again pulled her away, but this time he brought her up to a room, where he explained the situation.

"So, you're saying that you adopted them? And planned to do the same to all the names on your list?" Twilight dropped down onto the soft bed and eyed Ellio in disbelief.

"Yes," Ellio replied. The bed sank down as Ellio sat beside her. "It's my way of changing the future, and I need you here with me to make it work. Let's build a happy home with a bright future."

Twilight gazed into Ellio's sincere eyes and sighed. "Look, I admire you for doing all this, but I don't think I can build a family—"

Her words were stopped short when Ellio's lips were suddenly on hers. A conflicting feeling surged through her as their lips parted as fast as they'd touched. "I won't force you, Twilight, but think about it carefully. Live with me for at least six months. If you really can't see me as a man and can't accept my feelings, I'll give up and live my life as your brother." He stood up from the bed and left after saying that the room was for her.

For a while, she just sat there, feeling the breeze coming from the open window. It wasn't that she couldn't see Ellio as a man. Instead, she felt unfit to be his woman.

Part Three

Days melted into weeks, and weeks seamlessly transitioned into months. The seasons quickly changed, and before Twilight noticed, six months had gone. During that time, she grew fond of the young boys and often found herself yearning to become a part of the joyful home that Ellio had created. However, she knew that her dream must end sooner or later and that night, as Caldwell and Alfie were pulling both of her hands to read some stories with them, seemed to be the time.

"Caldwell, Alfie, could you just give me and Twilight some private time tonight?" Ellio asked.

"Why?" Alfie asked, but before Ellio could answer, Caldwell was already pulling him away.

Twilight laughed nervously. "He really acts like an older brother."

"Yeah, and they really adore you as their mother."

Twilight looked up at him but quickly averted her eyes from his loving gaze. "Could we talk someplace else?"

"Sure."

Twilight's heart constricted as they walked through the mansion corridor. It would be painful, but she must break it to him. She had to disappoint him for him to find someone better.

They seated themselves on the wire-framed chairs in the garden. Ellio simply sat silently beside Twilight as she took a couple of deep breaths and looked around her. She had lived in this decade for six months, too short time in comparison to eighteen painfully long years in the future. Yet, the place became more of a home, and the time she had spent with Ellio and his adopted sons had become so irreplaceable.

"Twilight—"

"Ellio, you're a great man, and I admit, it's bizarre to think about how you used to be younger, yet now I can't help but feel safe whenever I look at you." Ellio brightened up, but she raised her hand to stop him. "But I'm sorry."

"Sorry? What for? You love me, don't you?" He grasped her hand. "I know I might have come on a bit aggressively to you in the beginning, but I'm glad I waited. I promised that—"

"Ellio, I can't be your girlfriend, wife, or whatever term you want to use for a lover." Twilight attempted to remove her hand, but Ellio held it tight.

"Why?" he asked calmly.

When Twilight didn't reply, Ellio let go of her hand and cupped both of her cheeks, making her panic as he chased her eyes, forcing her to feel which of them was older and in control.

"Twilight, please, tell me so that I can decide whether to accept this rejection or not."

"You have to accept it! Because someone like you is better off with someone with a better background, someone more innocent than me."

Ellio chuckled and lightly bumped their foreheads together. "Background aside, I have never come across anyone with a heart as innocent as yours, Twilight. You're the purest girl any man could have."

Twilight opened her mouth to protest, but Ellio sealed her lips. A kiss, a long, forceful, but loving kiss that made her knees weak.

"And though I did say that I would live as your brother if you ever rejected me, know that if not you, I won't have anyone."

Tears blurred Twilight's eyes. "Are you sure you won't regret choosing me?"

Ellio smiled and kissed her again. "Twilight, my only regret is being unable to bring you to my side sooner."

"I..." she sniffed, fighting hard to say the words she'd been hiding for a long time.

"What?" Ellio asked with a triumphant spark in his brilliant blue eyes.

"I love you."

"You're just so adorable," he whispered and kissed her once before scooping her up and carrying her up to his bedroom. There, Twilight spent the most beautiful night of her life and woke up in the brightest daylight she'd ever seen.

"Good morning."

Twilight caressed Ellio's cheek and smiled. The world might have been a crappy place, but all that changed when he was by her side.

"Good morning."

What if the future is predetermined and nothing you do can change it?

All he wanted was to go back to the future, but that also meant living in a world without her.

If you're a fan of old crushes realized, age gap trope, and

romance that transcends time, then this book is for you.

—Read the first chapter on

the next page now!

Prologue

❦

JUST LIKE HIM

November 9th, 1955,

Alicante Jail

Eighteen-year-old Celestina gripped her handbag tighter as she stepped inside an eerie stone corridor, a single guard leading her toward one of the cells. He called through the bars to the man inside, who sat up on the metal bed and raised his head.

Celestina staggered back.

The guard put a gloved hand on her elbow. "¿Estás bien?"

She wanted to say "Si, I'm okay" and hide her emotion but her lips locked and her eyes widened when the prisoner turned his handsome oval face toward her. Her breath caught as her heartbeat sped up on seeing his dark-gray, hooded eyes—just as she remembered them from eleven years ago—but when a sneer appeared on his bow-shaped lips, she withered inside. This wasn't the same man who raised her.

He got to his feet and place his hand on the bar separating them. "¡Hola! Hermosita," he said, the disgusting smile never leaving his face.

She hated his insulting compliment. Hated how his eyes traveled down the length of her body. She struggled not to squirm, feeling as if an army of ants had crawled under her skin. But she endured it, looking him straight in the eyes. "¿Eres Ángel Castro Rivera?"

The man's face lit up, his leer widening into a menacing smile. "Si."

She swallowed, her throat sore from doing it so many times since leaving Beniardà. "Soy, Celestina. Hija de Maria Josefa De la Mota."

Ángel's smile faded for a second before returning. "Well," he drawled, his flirty tone gone, "daughter of Maria Josefa, why are you here?"

"I'm your daughter."

He looked at the guard, who shifted and turned toward the exit, but Celestina grabbed the hem of his uniform jacket, forcing him to stay.

Ángel sighed. "So, mi hija, what do you want from me?"

Good question. What did she want from him? Her mother turned thirty-three two months ago and, in her drunkenness, told her where her biological father was and that he looked just like her papá. And so, here she was after so much trouble proving her identity and so much preparation.

The corners of her eyes stung, and her stomach churned. Ángel not only looked like the man who lovingly raised her, he sounded just like him. And worse, they shared the same name.

Her mother warned her that this man, her father, would never care about her or why she existed. Maria Josefa was right, this man and her papá looked identical, but she was wrong about everything else. They were not the same at all. Her papá was caring, but this father in front of her was a criminal. A prisoner. Murderer. He'd taken multiple lives and was nothing like her papá.

What was she even doing here?

"I wouldn't mind having some fun with your body," he said as she turned on her heel, "just as I did with your mom. Although she was years younger than you then. She was what, uh, catorce? Si, si, she was fourteen. Oh, how good she felt."

Celestina turned back, raising her bag. Because of this brute, she never knew a mother's love. Because of him, both she and her mother suffered every day. She needed to hit him at least once to release years of pent-up anger. But the guard grabbed her arm.

"Time to go," he said.

"¡Monstruo! I hope you die here!" She almost growled as the guard pulled her away.

Want to read more?

Subscribe to my newsletter and read the next three chapters.

https://subscribepage.io/InAno therTimeSample

In Another Time: A time travel romance – release date: October 17, 2024

Love, Die, Live short trilogy
A story of loss, love and eincarnation

1: Live for Me | 2: Die for Me |
3: Love for Me

The Flame Squad series
Individual short stories of
he Flame Squad members, a
igilante group.
1: Sly Prince | 2: Shadow Prince
| 3: White Crow Princess

100% standalone short reads

Sweet Bloody Secret: A Short Vampire Romance
Under Her Spell: A short Christmas YA romance

About Jessie

Jessie Winterspring is a Filipina romance author who loves using tropes like found families, cheerful characters with dark experiences, goofy, adorkable, and brooding heroes/heroines. She mostly writes stories with time travel and paranormal elements.

Jessie often daydreams of traveling through time, but

since this dream is impossible, she did the next best thing. She writes them and sends her lucky characters on adventures that she should be having.

She wrote her first time-travel story, Fumes Variolas (not published), during National Novel Writing Month in 2013. However, In Another Time was the first story idea she came up with back in 2006. She wrote many other romances through the years before writing it down in 2019, using the next four years to edit it.

Jessie has a strong affection for animals and nature. She lives near the Mediterranean coast with her family and enjoys spending her time reading and falling in love with fictional characters. She also enjoys watching movies, Spanish telenovelas, Asian dramas, and anime while eating noodles with chopsticks or drooling over the 70s, 80s, and 90s music videos.

When she's not writing or reading, she usually spends her time on Instagram and occasionally posts stories on her blog.